pi•ra•nha

Fig. A

The piranha (/pɪɪɑːnə/) is a freshwater fish that lives in South American rivers. They are known for their sharp teeth, powerful jaws and their enormous appetite for meat.

The piranha will happily eat cows, sheep, donkeys, horses, monkeys, gorillas, cats, dogs, kittens, puppies, guinea pigs, bunny rabbits, goldfish, postmen, pizza delivery guys, little children who've been naughty, professional tennis players, old ladies who were just in the wrong place at the wrong time, little children who've actually been pretty good, astronauts, ballet dancers, belly dancers, TV talent show contestants, chimney sweeps and most other types of people.

What they don't eat, though, is fruit. Especially bananas.

PIRANHAS DON'T EAT BANANAS

For the Gravy Stains.

Scholastic Press
345 Pacific Highway Lindfield NSW 2070
An imprint of Scholastic Australia Pty Limited
PO Box 579 Gosford NSW 2250
ABN 11 000 614 577
www.scholastic.com.au

Part of the Scholastic Group
Sydney · Auckland · New York · Toronto · London · Mexico City
New Delhi · Hong Kong · Buenos Aires · Puerto Rico

Published by Scholastic Australia in 2015.
Text and illustrations copyright © Aaron Blabey, 2015.

National Library of Australia Cataloguing-in-Publication entry
Creator: Blabey, Aaron, author, illustrator.
Title: Piranhas don't eat bananas / Aaron Blabey (author + illustrator)
ISBN: 9781743625781 (hardback)
       9781743625798 (paperback)
Subjects: Piranhas—Juvenile fiction.
Dewey Number: A823.4

The artwork in this book is acrylic (with pens and pencils) on watercolour paper.

Typeset in Adobe Caslon.

Printed in China by Toppan Leefung Printing Ltd.
Scholastic Australia's policy, in association with Toppan Leefung, is to use papers that are renewable and made efficiently
from wood grown in responsibly managed forests, so as to minimise its environmental footprint.

20 19 18 17 16 15 14 13 12 11 10   18 19 20 / 1

PIRANHAS DON'T EAT BANANAS

AARON  BLABEY

A Scholastic Press book from Scholastic Australia

'Hey there, guys.
Would you like
a banana?'

'What's **wrong** with you, Brian?
You're a piranha.'

'Well,
how about some
silverbeet?'

'Are you serious, Brian?
We eat feet.'

'Or would you rather
a bowl of peas?'

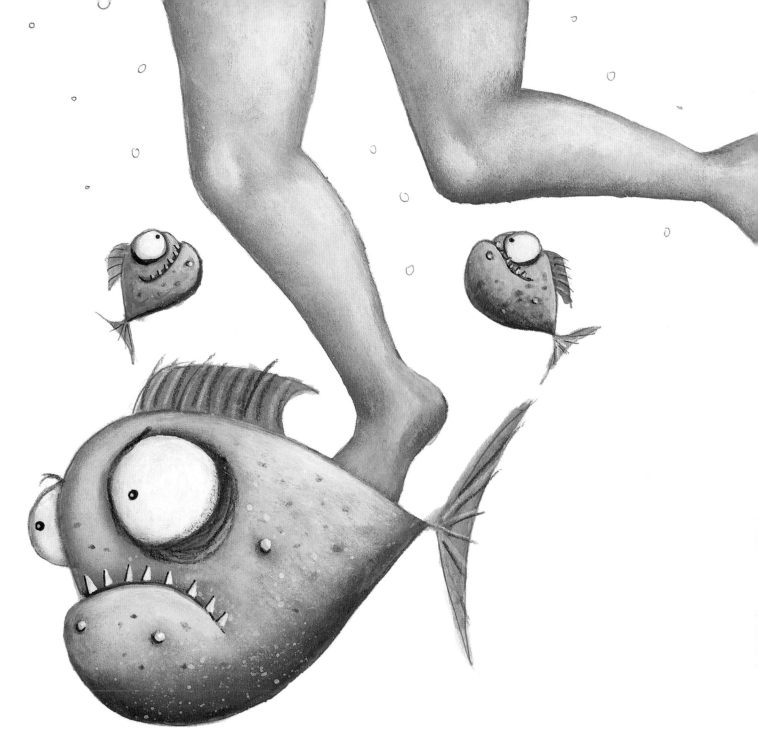

'Stop it, Brian.
We eat knees.'

'Well,
I bet you'd like some
juicy plums?'

'That's *it*, Brian! We eat bums!'

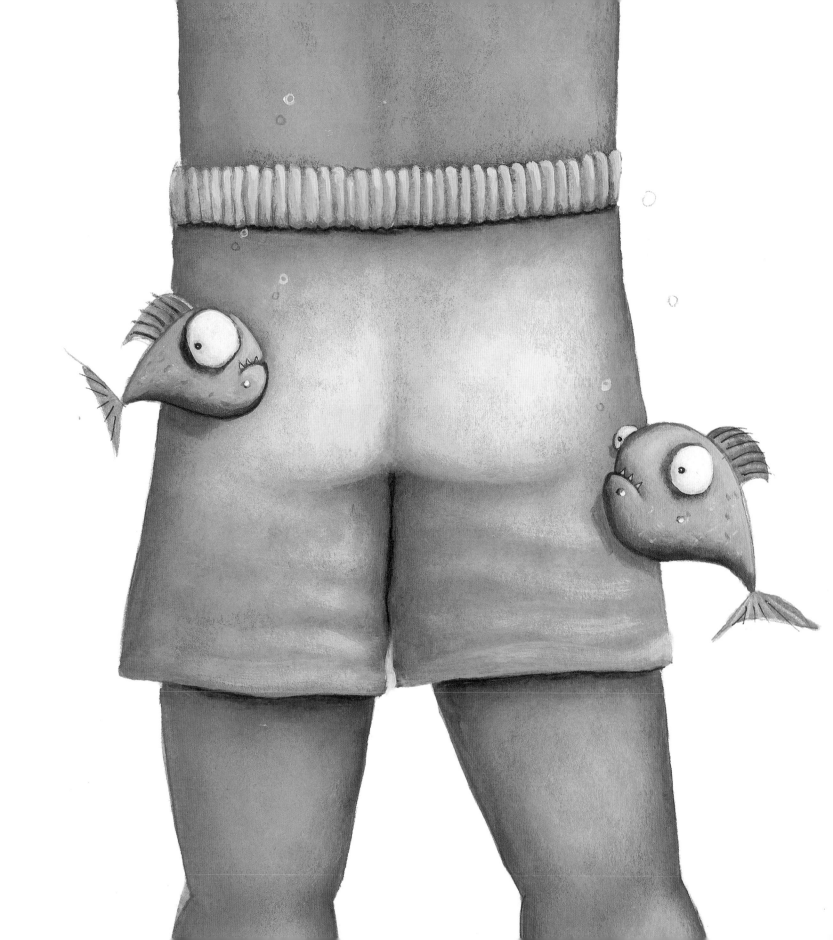

'We don't eat apples!

We don't eat beans!

We don't eat veggies!

We don't eat greens!

We don't eat melons!

We don't eat bananas!

And the reason
is simple, mate.

We are

PIRANHAS!'

'Well, I think that's silly, guys. Fruit is the best.'

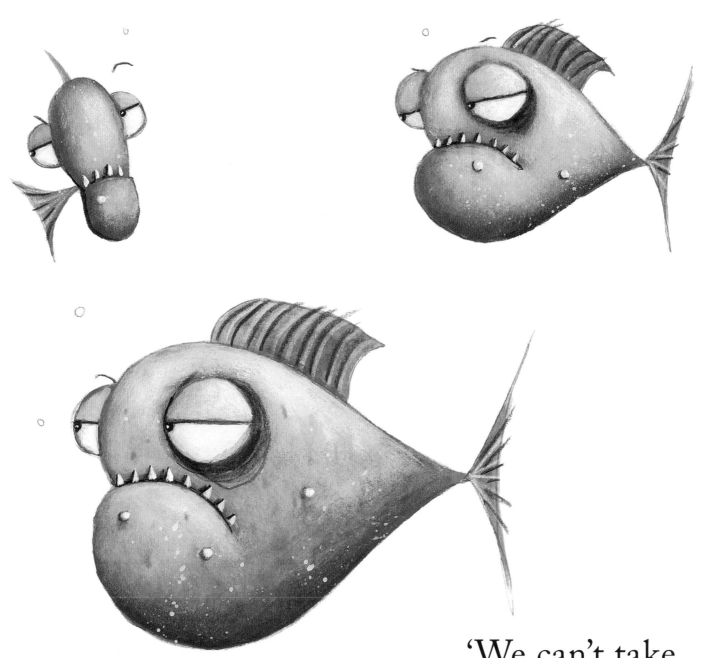

'We can't take
much more of this.
Give it a rest.'

'Okay, I'll stop then.
You'll hear no more chatter.

But ONLY if you try my
awesome fruit platter.'

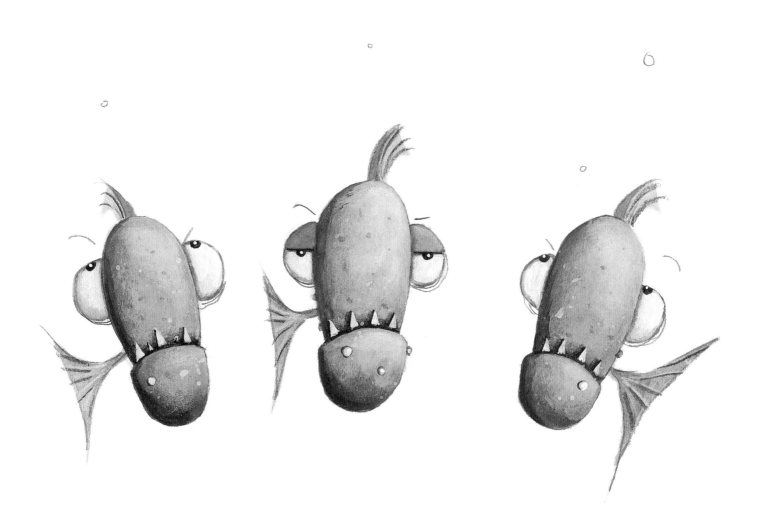

'Give it here, then.'

'So . . .

what do you think, guys?

Is it yucky or yum?'

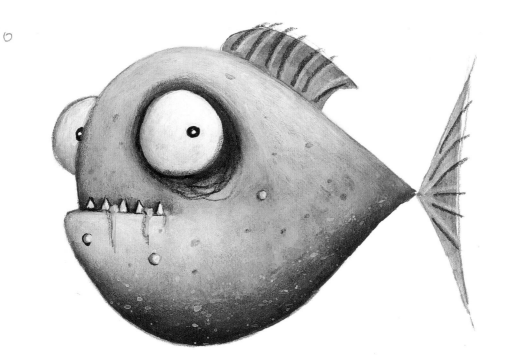

'It's very nice,
Brian . . .'

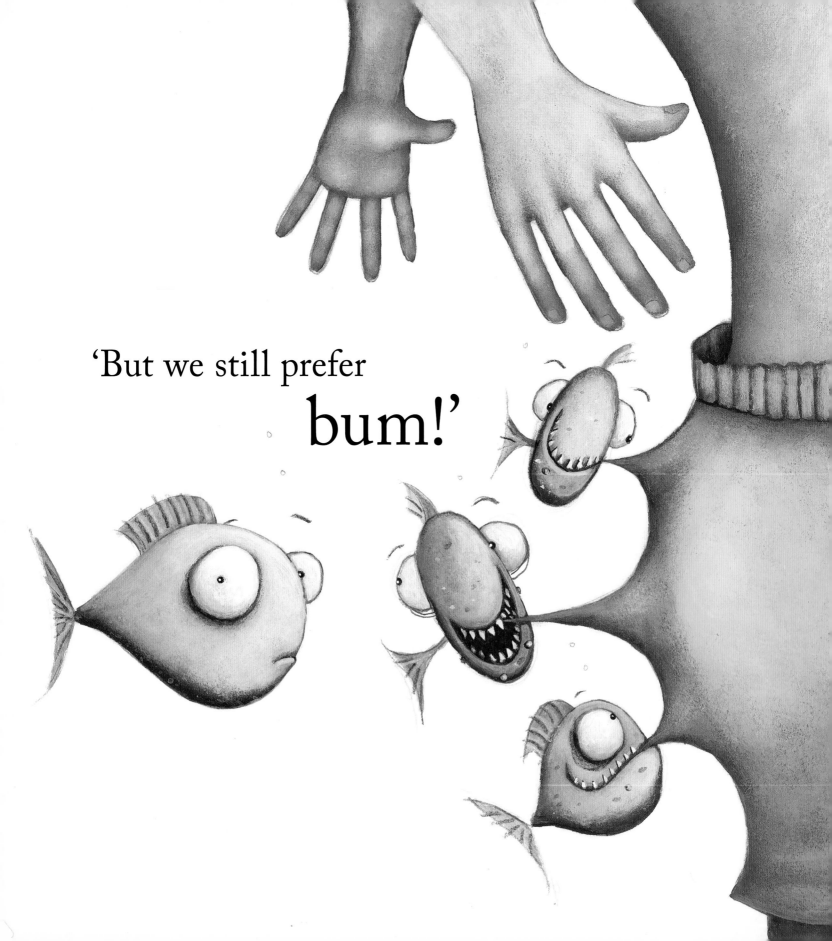

ba·na·na

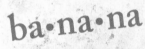

The banana is a long, curved, edible fruit grown on large flowering plants (*genus Musa*). They grow in clusters—generally in tropical or subtropical areas—and have soft pulpy flesh and yellow skin when ripe.

Fig. B

Bananas are often eaten and enjoyed by monkeys, chimpanzees, gorillas, orangutans, gibbons and people who don't mind the gooey texture. On the other hand, they are almost never eaten by South American river fish. Especially piranhas. That just doesn't happen.

Please note—the skin of a banana is very dangerous—you can slip on it, causing you to fall on your buttocks (/bu·m^/), which is possibly why piranhas avoid them.*

*Certainly, piranhas do not have buttocks. But they are intelligent and know to avoid dangerous fruits when they see them.